Thyme for Change
By: Lexie Hobby

ISBN-10: 0692854363
ISBN-13: 978-0692854365

Dedication
Written in loving memory of my papaw, Pete Hobby, a man who always encouraged me to use my God-given abilities.

Thyme for Change

Table of Contents

Thyme for Change

Thyme for Change

Chapter 1: Mountain Laurel

It was a frosty winter morning deep in the mountains of Rileni. The sun was just peeking from behind the horizon as a young woman in her early twenties exited her stone cottage. The chilly mountain breeze was nothing new to the reclusive herbalist. She had steeled herself against the cold long ago.

"I suppose I should visit the village today." the girl mused. "The change in season has probably gotten to a few people."

After pulling her scarf up to cover her nose, the young woman made her way to the small stable behind her cottage, her large Great Pyrenees -Snowball- moseying along behind her. There she kept her two horses -Stormy and Raj-, three hens and a rooster, and her four goats. She entered the stable and approached Raj, a beautiful dapple gray stallion and stroked his velvety-soft nose.

"Do you feel up for a ride today, Raji-boy?" She asked, reaching for a comb to brush the horse's mane.

Raj whinnied in response and seemed to answer her question with a bob of his head as he exhaled through his nose. The blonde-haired girl laughed and kissed his nose before going about her daily routine of feeding the animals before letting them out into the small pasture for the day.

"Okay, Snowball, time to go to work." the young woman announced, followed by a quick whistle.

The large dog's ears perked up. He rose from his sitting position near the entrance and trotted out the back door to follow the livestock into the pasture. He herded the goats and chickens together, making sure none of them wandered off.

With that chore done, the young blonde went back to Raj's stall and saddled him for her trip to the village. She packed a saddlebag full of medicinal herbs, salves, and drinkable medicines to help the villagers. In another, she packed a canteen of water and some snacks for her and Raj to eat along the way.

"Alright, Raji-boy, off we go." She said, coaxing the stallion to a trotting pace as they wove down the mountain trail.

Meanwhile, in the small village about two miles from the base of the mountain, many of the children had gathered around one of the elders. He was telling them tales from generations past. He stopped when he saw the familiar honey-blonde hair, sky blue eyes, and fair complexion of a young herbalist trotting into town on her gray stallion.

"Look there, children. Take care you don't cross that young woman's path. That girl is a witch. She'll put a curse on you if you anger her." The old man warned.

"Is she really a witch?" A young boy questioned. "She looks like a nice lady to me."

"She's a witch alright. She was born here in this village. Not long after she was born, both her parents died of a plague. It spread to several others. Her grandmother was long thought to be a witch as well. After the death of her son and daughter-in-law, she took her granddaughter into the mountains to teach her all of her witch-like ways." The old man answered. "Stay away from Laurel the Witch."

Laurel dismounted and tied Raj to a hitching post. Several people stopped to stare at her, some in awe, some with suspicion. Her beauty was unnatural, not to mention she lived alone in the mountains and made medicine for a living. Those facts alone were enough to make the overly superstitious villagers wary of her.

'There they go again. You'd think they'd get used to seeing me after all these years.' Laurel thought with a sigh as she unpacked one of the saddlebags.

"E-Excuse me, m-miss." A middle age woman stammered.

"Yes? How can I help you today?" Laurel replied, smiling kindly at the older woman.

"O-One of my children has a cold. D-Do you have anything for that?"

"Of course. I anticipated a few would catch colds because of the change in season. I have just the thing."

Laurel pulled out a small paper envelope

with some crushed herbs inside: Echinacea to relieve cold-like symptoms, Sage to soothe sore throats, and Thyme to help coughing. She handed the envelope to the woman.

"Just brew some tea and stir about a fourth of that in with it. Give your child one dose a day for four days. That should take care of the cold. If not, come up to my cottage, and I'll give you some more." Laurel explained.

"Th-Thank you very much. Here." The woman shoved a few gold coins into Laurel's hands before hurrying away.

"Oh, this it too mu-!" Laurel tried to protest, but the woman was already out of sight. *'The medicine only cost one gold coin...'*

Only those truly desperate for medicine dared to approach Laurel. Everyone in the village thought she was a witch. They always paid her way too much as well, for fear of angering her. Laurel tried to be as friendly as she could, but no one looked her in the eyes, no one smiled at her, and absolutely no one came to visit her.

'Granny warned me the villagers would be like this, but...I thought I could get them to warm up to me if I was friendly...' Laurel

thought as she packed up and prepared to head home. *'I guess I shouldn't be surprised. It's been like this for as long as I can remember...'*

"Look, look! There goes Laurel the witch!" A small child whispered to his friend, but his attempted whisper wasn't very effective.

"Shhh! She'll hear you!" The other whispered back. "Do you want her to put a curse on you?!"

"Curses don't exist, little ones. You're only cursed if you think you are." Laurel said, trying her best to hide the fact that their words hurt her. *'If anyone is cursed...it's me.'*

"She heard us! Let's get outta here!" the second child exclaimed, grabbing the other's wrist and dragging him away.

Laurel glanced sadly at the village one last time before beginning the journey up the mountain. While she was in the village, she heard whispers about other things besides her for a change. Many of the villagers mentioned the stirrings of war at the northern border. The rumors were unsettling, to say the least.

'Maybe I should...offer my services.' Laurel pondered. *'Lord, am I still needed here? Or are*

you calling me somewhere else?'

Chapter 2: The General of Rileni

On the same day in another part of Rileni, a young general was preparing his troops for battle. A neighboring land had recently been trying to occupy more and more of Rileni land. General Alrik Northstride had been given full permission from the king to attack as he saw fit.

"General Northstride, sir. I have the reports from the scouts you sent into enemy territory, sir." A soldier announced, saluting his superior.

"Good. It's about time. What's the status on those barbarians?" Alrik inquired.

"Sir, they have troops stationed all along the river that divides our two countries. Since we arrived, they haven't set foot outside their base camp located just south of our current location, but they're getting bolder by the day. It's like they're waiting for something."

"Waiting for something, eh?....Well, we'll attack before whatever it is gets there. Tell all the men to grab their weapons. We'll launch a surprise attack tonight as soon as it gets dark."

"Yes, sir!"

The soldier left the tent, leaving Alrik to his own thoughts. He ran a hand through his auburn hair and sighed, an action not fitting for someone so young, but the strains of the battlefield had taken their toll on him.

His handsome face was hidden by a thick beard, unruly because of how long he'd been in the field, and an old scar that stretched from between his right ear and eye, across his cheek to the base of his jaw. It was a souvenir from his first battle. Since that day, whenever he was ab-out to do battle, that scar would begin to tingle, as if it was reminding him not to be careless.

'*I won't be careless. I have everything planned out. I left no room for error. No barbarian will get the better of me.*' Alrik told himself.

With that thought in mind, he rose to his feet and put on his helmet to complete his suit of armor. Before exiting his tent, he grabbed his shield and made sure his sword was securely strapped to his back.

As Alrik walked through the encampment, he overheard many of the young soldiers talking about their new wives or sweethearts they'd left in their hometowns that they promised to marry when they returned home. He was used to hearing that kind of thing. A few years ago, he would probably have joined in, but many things had changed.

The words of the woman he once loved rang in his ears.

"Alrik, I love you, but I can't marry you," Marie stated. "I can't marry a man who's already married."

"But Marie, I'm n-" Alrik tried to protest.

"To his job." Marie finished.

"Marie, I can change. Just give me a chance!"

But his words fell on deaf ears. Marie had turned and began walking away, her wavy, raven-colored hair blowing in the slight breeze. Her words stung, far more than any injury Alrik had received in battle.

Alrik took her advice. He took a leave of

absence from the front lines a week. He succeeded in staying home and relaxing the first day.

The next day, he went to tell Marie the good news, but he saw her with another man. Their arms linked as he led her through town. He even had the audacity to peck her on the cheek. Marie blushed and giggled. Alrik left without saying a word.

'You loved me, did you? As if I'd believe that. You only said that until you found a better deal. Well, I'll show you. I'll show the whole world! I am Alrik Northstride! I'll become someone so great you'll rue the day you stomped on my heart!' Alrik vowed.

After that day, Alrik scarcely took a leave of absence. He climbed up the ranks faster than anyone had in the history of Rileni. Before he knew it, he was the king's most trusted general. Even though he was only in his late twenties, Alrik had already given up all hope of getting married.

'It's not like I would want to anyway. I learned my lesson. I don't want to go through that again. Trusting in others only leads to

heartbreak.' Alrik thought to himself, blocking out the chatter from the other soldiers.

When the soldiers noticed his arrival, they immediately stopped their chatting and stood at attention, ready to receive their orders. Alrik passed them by without so much as a glance, his head held high and his eyes never wavering from the path in front of him.

"General Northstride sir, I've prepared your horse for battle." A commander announced.

"Horses won't be necessary. We'll be going on foot." Alrik replied.

"Sir?"

"Horses make too much noise. In order to pull off a surprise attack on a heavily guarded border and base camp, we need the element of surprise."

"Yes, sir! I'll spread the word to the rest of the troops right away."

The commander led the horse back to the makeshift stable and then went about the camp informing the other soldiers.

As the sun began to set behind the mountains, the soldiers gathered around Alrik to await further instruction.

"Men, we were sent here by King William Armand V to take care of the barbarians that keep invading our land from the North. We are protecting our homeland, our friends, our families, and above all, our faith! Don't relent when the enemy bears down on you! Fight back! You are Rileni's finest warriors!" Alrik declared, unsheathing his sword and thrusting it into the air.

"Yes, sir!" the collective answers from every soldier in camp replied.

"Then onward! May God give us victory!"

The soldiers followed Alrik to the river that divided Rileni with the Barbarians of the North. There was no sign of the enemy, so the soldiers waded across the river, heavy armor and all. Alrik had picked that spot to cross the river because it was the safest; the other parts of the river would be impossible due to the strong currents.

"This is it, men. The barbarians' base camp isn't far now. Stay on your guard." Alrik warned.

The soldiers nodded in understanding as they pushed their way through the thick forest along the riverbank. Some looked out at the swirling currents of the river with fear. Others didn't dare to. Alrik glanced at the river, but he paid it no mind and focused on the task at hand.

The sudden snapping of a twig instantly put him on alert. He signaled to his men to stop and be silent. Before anyone had time to react, several hooded figures jumped down from the trees and attacked, some with blow darts, others with small daggers.

"Soldiers of Rileni, attack!!!" Alrik commanded, unsheathing his sword to block the attack of one of the hooded figures.

He easily overpowered the smaller built man and sent him flying with one powerful kick to the ribs, only to be attacked by another hooded stranger.

There were many more hooded figures than Rileni soldiers, but they made up for it in strength and skill. It wasn't long before all the attackers laid on the ground, either dead or too wounded to continue.

'Something doesn't add up...We won too easily.' Alrik thought, placing a hand on his chin, wracking his brain for anything that seemed off.

The soldiers continued on to the enemy base. Alrik still felt uneasy about their earlier triumph. He ran through several scenarios in his head, hoping to uncover the enemy's plans, but no matter how many he tried, he came up short.

'*We'll just have to play it by ear then.*' Alrik concluded. 'I've trained my men for times like these. They won't disappoint me.'

"General, I just scouted the area up ahead. We're fast approaching the camp. There are no walls or permanent structures of any kind. It's lying right next to the riverbank wide open for an attack. Several barbarians are awake, waiting for us." A scout informed.

"I suppose the element of surprise is out of the question now...Very well. We'll attack head on. Hold nothing back." Alrik stated. "But be vigilant."

"Yes, sir!"

The company of soldiers charged the camp. The barbarians were waiting, swords brandished and ready to attack. The Rileni soldiers, eager to prove themselves after being taken by surprise, rushed ahead of Alrik to engage them in combat.

Alrik was surprised at their eagerness to do battle, but he let them handle the front lines while he and some of the other senior warriors handled the few barbarians that managed to break through. The ones that did were decent warriors. One even got a lucky shot, slightly grazing Alrik under the breastplate of his armor.

"Keep it up, men! We've got them cornered! Show no mercy!" Alrik barked.

No sooner were those words out of his mouth than a small explosion was heard. Alrik froze, sheathed his sword, and looked around to see where the noise had come from.

A second later another, closer, explosion sent him tumbling down the riverbank. His body collided with several rocks on the way down. He heard a pop, and something snapped. An intense pain soon followed.

Before he fell into the river, he caught a glimpse of his soldiers holding up their swords in victory over the barbarians, completely unaware of his absence. The currents of the river soon took him. One last thought entered his mind before he blacked out.

'We won...That's all that matters.'

Chapter 3: Crossing Paths

Laurel got up bright and early the morning after her excursion to the village. After doing her usual morning chores like feeding the animals, she gathered all her dirty clothes and placed them in a basket. She planned on going to the river to wash them. It was a bit of a trek down the mountain, so she rode Stormy.

"It's much easier to go up and down the mountain with you and Raj, Stormy." Laurel praised, ruffling the silver and white mare's mane affectionately.

Stormy neighed in response and held her head higher as if she was proud of herself. Laurel giggled and dismounted as they had almost reached the river. She held Stormy's reins in one hand and parted the thick foliage with the other.

"Doing laundry in winter is the wor-" Laurel

stopped when she saw something at the edge of the river.

She held her hand to shield the morning sun from her eyes as she neared the mysterious mass lying on the bank. She let out a sharp gasp and dropped Stormy's reins when she saw what it was.

An auburn-haired man had washed up on the bank, his hand holding tightly to the hilt of a sword stuck deep in the soft soil like he'd used it to drag himself on shore. Laurel rushed over and knelt beside the man.

"Sir, what happened to you?! Let me help!" Laurel offered, trying to help the man to his feet.

"Don't...touch me, girl...These injuries...are nothing." The man rasped, smacking her hand away, rather weakly despite how muscular he was.

"Pardon my forwardness, but they don't *look* like nothing. Let me help. I'm the closest thing to a doctor there is around here," Laurel replied, ignoring the man's protests that he was fine. "Stormy, c'mere."

Stormy trotted over at Laurel's call. Laurel, despite her small frame, managed to hoist the ill-tempered man onto Stormy's back. He was too weak to sit up, so he laid on her with his arms and legs dangling over on either side of her.

"I don't know what happened, but you were obviously in some kind of battle and either fell, or were thrown, into the river. In this cold weather, it's a wonder you're still alive." Laurel commented, trying to keep the shivering man awake until she got him to her cottage. "You must be quite stubborn."

"How...dare you talk...to me like that. Do you know...who I am?" The man wheezed.

"As a matter of fact, I don't. Who are you? Where are you from? How did you end up washed up on the riverbank?" Laurel persisted.

"I...am General Alrik Northstride. I'm from the capital...and how I ended up like this...is none...of your...business."

"Wow, a general, huh?" Laurel whistled. "Now I really wanna know how you got so roughed up. It must have been quite the accident."

"It was...the barbarians...There were small explosives planted in the ground...One went off ...near me...I was knocked into the river....

Happy, now?”

"I'll be happy when I have your injuries taken care of. Just stay awake until you get warmed up. I don't want you dying of hypothermia before we get to my cottage.”

"You're...a strange woman...”

"I get that a lot.”

It was slow going, but eventually, they reached Laurel's cottage. Laurel quickly tied Stormy to one of the support beams of her front porch and helped Alrik dismount.

"Can you walk?” Laurel asked.

"Of...course I ca-” Alrik stopped short when a sharp pain shot up his left leg the moment it touched the ground.

Laurel quickly slipped one of his arms around her shoulder to support him. It was then she noticed the slice in his armor. It wasn't very deep, but there was definitely an open wound. The leather and cloth around the slice was stained red with blood.

"You're in worse shape than I thought. I'd better hurry.” Laurel said, helping Alrik into her home.

"Silence...I didn't...ask for your help.” Alrik

coughed.

"You don't have to ask in order to receive help. I see a need, so I'm going to fill it. Think about it this way, Mr. General, if you were in a situation where you had to act before being asked to in order to save countless lives, you would do it. Besides, if everyone waited to be asked to do something, nothing would get done." Laurel replied. "Now, first thing's first, I need to bandage up that wound under your breastplate. You'll need to remove it."

Alrik didn't respond for a minute. He just glared up at the golden blonde-haired girl in front of him from where she had sat him on a chair in a small bedroom. Finally, after a bit of grumbling, he complied.

Laurel tied her hair back and began examining the shallow cut. It wasn't anything to worry about, but if left alone it might get infected. She wetted a washcloth and removed the dried blood, dirt, and unclean river water. Next, she applied a cream with lavender, to act as an antiseptic, and lemon balm, to help the healing process.

"All right, lean forward a bit." Laurel

instructed, grabbing a roll of bandages.

"...Pardon?" Alrik questioned.

"Lean. Forward." Laurel repeated, firmer than before. "I need to wrap your wound."

"I...am General Alrik Northstride of the Rileni...Royal Army...You can't order me like that."

Laurel sighed, pinched the bridge of her nose, and closed her eyes for a second before opening them again. She placed her hands on her hips and looked Alrik directly in his emerald green eyes without flinching.

"Right now, you are not a general. You are my patient. If you want to get well as quickly as possible, do as I say." Laurel stated firmly. "Trust me. I know what I'm doing."

'*Who is this woman? Who does she think she is?*' Alrik thought as he begrudgingly did as he was told.

Laurel wrapped the bandages snuggly around Alrik's middle then shoved a sprig of dried lavender in his mouth. He gave her a quizzical look.

"To help calm you down. I have a feeling this next part might be a little painful." Laurel explained, rolling up the leg of his pants to examine his injured leg. "Yeah, I thought so. It's broken."

Alrik's eyes widened. A broken bone meant an incredibly long recovery period. There wasn't much he could do about it though. His leg was broken. He wouldn't be able to get very far if he tried to escape, and he could feel himself getting weaker by the minute. His head was throbbing, and his eyelids were burning with fatigue.

"Once I'm done, you should change out of those wet clothes. I think my grandmother kept some of my father's old clothes. You can wear those." Laurel said after positioning his leg and using a stick to keep it aligned while she wrapped it tightly. "Now...what other injuries are there?"

"I'm fine. Why should I tell you anything?"

"If you don't tell me, I'll have to find them myself, and it would take much longer and be more painful."

"...Left shoulder and lower right arm."

"That's better."

After examining the places Alrik had told her, Laurel found that his left shoulder had popped out of the socket, and his right radius was fractured.

"Man, you must have hit every rock before falling into the river." Laurel commented. "I don't think I've ever seen a person this injured before. Did you hit your head too?"

"It's possible." Alrik admitted, avoiding Laurel's gaze.

"Well, I'll look at it later. I'm about to pop your shoulder back into place. You might wanna hold onto the arm of the chair or something."

Before Alrik could do that, he felt a sharp pain as his shoulder popped back into place. He made a strangled choking sound, clenching his teeth to keep from yelling out in pain.

"A little more warning would have been nice." Alrik wheezed through gritted teeth.

"Sorry 'bout that, but it's better if you're not expecting it." Laurel explained.

Next, Laurel bandaged the general's fractured arm, making sure the bone wasn't protruding from the skin before wrapping it up to keep it firmly in place.

After she finished treating all the visible wounds, including a minor bump on his temple, Laurel placed a hand on Alrik's forehead to check his temperature. It was higher than normal, but it wasn't too alarming at that moment.

"I've treated all the injuries I can see, but you're not out of the woods just yet. I don't know how long you were in that river, but it was long enough to put you in danger of hypothermia. I'll need to keep you under observation for the next couple days." Laurel explained, handing him a stack of her father's old clothes. "Now change into these. I'll go get you a towel to dry your hair and make something to warm you up."

"Why are you doing all this? I'm a total stranger." Alrik questioned, raising an eyebrow skeptically. "What do you stand to gain from helping me? I could be lying to you about being a general. I could be a wanted killer for all you know."

"Well, you were injured...I wasn't just going to leave you to die there. I read about a similar situation in the Bible. A man was beaten, robbed, and left for dead on the side of the road. No one would help him until a person from an enemy people group that is. He treated his wounds, put him on his own donkey, carried him to an inn, and paid for the innkeeper to take care of him.

This was a parable told by Jesus about how we should treat our neighbors. I'm only doing what the Bible says." Laurel paused for a moment and thought about his second point. "As for how I know you're not lying to me, I can just pick up on those sorts of things. Call it a...trick of the trade."

Before Alrik could respond, Laurel left the small bedroom, the one that used to belong to her grandmother, and shut the door behind her. Alrik stared at the closed door for a moment, unsure of how to respond. Other than his own mother, no woman had ever been that kind to him, without expecting something in return.

'The Bible, huh? How long has it been since...I read mine?' Alrik thought, suddenly yearning to read it after ten long years.

Alrik shook that thought away. In an effort to get changed before Laurel returned, Alrik did his best to hurry, but with a broken leg, a fractured arm, and a newly realigned shoulder, it was a bit difficult. He managed it, however, and no sooner had he buttoned the shirt than a knock came at the door.

"Can I come in?" Laurel asked.

"...Yeah." Alrik replied, feeling a bit

awkward.

Laurel opened the door and came in with a towel flung over one shoulder and a tray of tea and hot oatmeal in her hands. Considering all he'd had for the past two weeks was military rations of bread and dried meat, a hot meal was like heaven for Alrik.

After he finished eating, Laurel felt Alrik's forehead again. His cheeks were a bit flushed, but the rest of his face wasn't as pale as when she'd found him. It was definitely an improvement.

"Alright, time for you to get some rest." Laurel announced, taking the empty tray and placing it on a nearby table.

She walked over to the neatly made bed and pulled back the quilt and sheets. The sweet lemon and lavender scent her grandmother had always worn drifted into her nose. For a split-second, Laurel froze. Memories of her grandmother flashed before her eyes, making her tear up a little. She shook her head to clear it and turned back to Alrik.

"I don't want you putting any pressure on your leg for the next few days, so if you need anything, just call. I'll be in and out of here checking up on you." Laurel explained, blinking back the tears that stung the corners of her eyes.

"I don't need you looking after me like a small child. I'm a grown man." Alrik mumbled, trying to stifle a yawn.

"Yeah, yeah, you're General Alrik North-something-or-other. I get it." Laurel giggled, rolling her eyes.

"Northstride." Alrik corrected.

"Mhm, yeah that. I'm Laurel by the way, Laurel Meyers, the best dang herbalist around."

Laurel helped support Alrik as she guided him to the bed. He got in with little trouble. As soon as his head hit the pillow, he was out like a light. Laurel sighed in relief and put an extra blanket over him.

'*Just in case.*' She told herself before leaving the room.

Chapter 4: Putting Pride Aside

Once Laurel left Alrik to rest, she busied herself around the house, cleaning, making medicine, and other important tasks.

'He'll need something to help him walk for a while...' Laurel thought. *'Maybe Granny's old cane is around here somewhere...'*

Laurel dug around in the closet she had stored all her grandmother's important things until she found what she was looking for.

"Here it is." Laurel stated, examining the wooden cane her grandmother used in her later years. "It might be a bit short for him though...I guess I'll just go find a longer one in the woods."

Laurel returned the cane to its rightful place. Many of her grandmother's treasures surrounded it. Staring at them brought back many fond memories, but her grandmother's death added a bitterness to the sweetness of them. Before she could get too lost in the past, Laurel stood up and shut the door.

"I don't have time for that right now." She told herself, rubbing her face with her hands. "Granny would probably tell me something like, 'Laurel honey, if you have a job to do, then do it' or 'Laurel, don't waste time mourning when you know God has something more important for you to do'."

Laurel looked outside and saw that the sky was beginning to darken. Gray clouds hid the sun from view. It looked like a snowstorm if she ever saw one. She ran outside and called for Snowball to herd the animals back into the stable.

"Snowball, let's go, sweet boy." Laurel cooed after securing the stable. "You're coming inside with me."

Snowball wagged his tail happily as he followed Laurel back to the house. Once inside, Snowball tilted his head to one side curiously and approached the closed door to her grandmother's bedroom. He sniffed under the door and looked back at Laurel as if saying, "You know there's someone in there, right?"

"We'll be having a guest staying with us for a while, Snowball." Laurel explained, kneeling to pet him. "I found him by the river this morning. He was in pretty bad shape, so I brought him back here."

Snowball scooted closer and placed a paw on her knee as he looked up at her with big, chocolate-brown eyes. Laurel wrapped her arms around the large, fluffy dog and buried her face in his soft fur. It was like Snowball could read her mind. He knew exactly what to do.

"You're a good boy, Snowball. Such a good boy. You are truly a gift from God." Laurel murmured. "My heart is racing. It's been so long since I've actually had someone to talk to other than the villagers."

A few hours passed. Laurel checked in on Alrik periodically. She was concerned about his steadily rising temperature.

"I guess a fever is better than hypothermia, but..." Laurel trailed off as Alrik began to stir.

Alrik opened his eyes and blinked a couple of times, looking confused at his unfamiliar surroundings for a moment. His eyes drifted to Laurel who was standing to his right.

"What is it, woman?" He muttered, voice thick from sleep.

"How do you feel. You have a bit of a fever. Is there anything else I should know about? Headaches? Chills? Sore throat?" Laurel replied, pulling up a chair and sitting down.

"You needn't concern yourself with me. I'm fine."

Laurel couldn't help but notice he flinched and closed one eye when he spoke.

"So, you have a headache as well then?" She inquired.

"How did you--?"

"When you've been doing this as long as I have, you pick up a few things here and there." Laurel stood up. "Well, I'm going to go make you some medicine. I'll be right back."

Laurel exited the room and went into the kitchen. On the longest wall, she had shelves upon shelves of dried herbs and other medicinal plants and flowers, all in their own labeled containers. She picked a few jars from the shelf and scooped some of the contents of each into a small bowl. Next, she ground them up a bit more and put the mixture in some chamomile and mint tea.

While she was doing this, Snowball sauntered into the bedroom where Alrik was and rested his chin on the bed next to Alrik's face.

"...Hello there." Alrik greeted, unsure how to respond to the large fluffy dog. Snowball tilted his head to one side then jumped on the bed and curled up to Alrik's left, resting his large head on Alrik's stomach. When Laurel returned, she stopped dead in her tracks as soon as she entered the room. She put her hand over her mouth to keep from laughing.

"I take it this oversized ball of fluff is yours?" Alrik asked, sounding much less gruff than before.

"Yes. That's my Snowball. He's very sweet, smart too." Laurel replied, setting the tray on the bedside table. "Aren't you, boy?"

Snowball's ears perked up, but other than that, he made no effort to move from his position. Just having him in the room put both Laurel and Alrik at ease. Something about the large white dog was calming. Maybe it was his laid-back attitude or his fluffy white fur that resembled a cloud drifting lazily across the sky. It was so calming in fact that both Alrik and Laurel lost their trains of thought and sat there in silence for a moment.

"Oh right! The medicine!" Laurel remembered, getting up from her seat and grabbing the teacup of medicine. "Here, drink this. It'll help bring down your fever."

To Laurel's surprise, Alrik took the cup with his left hand and drank every last drop without a single word of complaint. Laurel smiled and took the cup when he finished.

"If it's just a fever, it should be gone by tomorrow. I put some Echinacea flowers in the tea, so if you caught a cold or the flu, it should lessen the symptoms or stop them entirely. It all depends on how much rest you get." Laurel explained. "So, unless you want to be stuck in bed for a week or more, I suggest you take it easy."

"I'm a general. Taking it easy isn't in my vocabulary." Alrik replied.

"Well, you better put it in your vocabulary, or you'll have a very angry herbalist to deal with." Laurel teased, doing her best to look intimidating.

"I'll take my chances."

"How about this. I'll find you a walking stick to use when your fever goes down. That way you don't have to stay cooped up all day."

"You drive a hard bargain...but I think I can manage."

"Good. I didn't want to be the angry herbalist if I could help it." Laurel stood and turned to leave. "I'll let you rest for a bit. Just call me if you need anything, or send Snowball."

"Sure."

Laurel left the room, leaving the door open just enough for Snowball to slip out if he needed to. She put on her coat and scarf and prepared to go out to look for a walking stick before the snowstorm hit.

To avoid being caught out in the storm, Laurel limited her search radius to a five minutes' walk from her cottage. The foliage of the forest around her mountaintop cottage was sparse, so it was easy to keep an eye on the sky as she walked.

There were many different kinds of trees growing in the forest, but the majority of them were birch trees. Their pearly-white bark with dark streaks scattered across in various patterns was beautiful. There were tons of them to choose from, but the tree that always drew Laurel's attention was the lone cherry tree that stood on a small bluff overlooking the river below.

Ever since she could remember, that cherry tree had always been a special place for her. She had climbed it countless times as she got older, and though one wrong move could have doomed her, she never felt scared when she sat on one of its branches with her feet dangling over. In the spring and fall its beautiful pale pink flowers danced in the wind, spreading their sweet scent wherever the breeze took them.

When Laurel approached the old tree, she found a small limb that had fallen. It was about her height with a few twigs growing from the top and about as big around as a broom handle. It would make a perfect walking stick for the bedridden general.

"Thank you, old friend." Laurel murmured, gazing up at the bare branches of her favorite tree.

Laurel hurried back to her cottage and began smoothing out the surface of the limb with a small carving knife. She threw the bark and excess twigs into a jar, planning to empty them after the snowstorm passed. From where she sat near the fireplace, she could see the red-orange hues of the sun setting behind the mountain outside her window.

"Today passed quickly...I guess having another human being to talk to will have that effect." She mused. "It feels...nice."

Chapter 5: Wounds of the Past

'Where am I? Why does my body feel like it's on fire? It's hard to breathe…There's nothing around me but darkness. Why…Why can't I see anything?' I thought desperately.

"Alrik…Alrik?" A familiar voice called.

"Marie…Marie is that you? Where are you?" I called back, looking around wildly.

Marie suddenly came into view. Her body looked like it was coated in light. She held out her hand to me, a warm smile on her delicate face. I tried to reach out to her, but it seemed like the closer I got, the farther away she receded.

"Marie, wait! Wait for me!" I begged.

Before I could blink, Marie's face was inches from mine, but her smile was gone. In its' place was a sinister smirk, and her eyes looked at me in disgust, as if I was nothing more than *something meant to be thrown away.*

"Why would I wait for you? I don't love you. I never loved you, Alrik. I was leading you on the entire time. Saying you were married to your job was just an excuse to get rid of you so I could move on to someone better." Marie spat, slapping my hand away.

I stood there in shock as she turned, with a spring in her step, and ran to the outstretched arms of the man that I'd seen her with ten years ago.

"Why, Marie...? Why did you betray me?!" I shouted.

"Alrik...Alrik, wake up!" Laurel pleaded, gently shaking the sleeping general.

Alrik pushed himself up abruptly but recoiled when pain shot up his injured right arm. Laurel caught him before he could fall backward and hit his head on the headboard.

"Alrik, are you all right?" Laurel asked, eyes wide with fright and worry.

Alrik was drenched in sweat, and his breathing was slow and raspy, like he'd just run a marathon. His eyes were wild and unfocused, as if the nightmare still had him in its grasp.

"Marie...?" Alrik rasped.

"No, it's me, Laurel." Laurel murmured, gently lowering his head back onto the pillow and pulling up the blankets.

"Laurel?" Alrik questioned, blinking a few times to clear his vision.

"Yeah. I'm right here. Snowball came and got me...I'm glad he did. Your fever spiked, but now it's returning to normal. You should be fine now."

"...Thank you."

"You're welcome....So, who's Marie? Sweetheart? Fiance?...Wife?"

"She's no one important...not anymore anyway." Alrik replied gruffly, looking away.
Laurel sat down in the chair next to Alrik and placed her hand on top of his.

"I'm sorry. I shouldn't have asked." Laurel apologized. "You need to concentrate on getting well, not dwelling on the past."

"No, it's alright. It's been ten years...I should be over it by now." Alrik sighed.

"...I can't make a medicine for a broken heart. You just have to endure it until God closes the wounds others have left behind." Laurel squeezed Alrik's hand. "But I can be there to talk if you ever feel up to it."

"I'll...sleep on it."

"Okay. Sleep is good. I'll see you in the morning."

"Yeah..."

A week passed by in the blink of an eye, for Laurel anyway. With all the snow, Laurel had kept Alrik indoors to keep him from slipping on the ice and injuring himself further. She gave him the sanded and polished walking stick after three days of bed rest and let him walk laps around the living room, but he was getting more restless by the hour.

One day, while Laurel was out taking care of the animals, Alrik seized the opportunity, grabbed the walking stick, and made a beeline for the door. Once outside on the porch, he got his first good look at his surroundings since he'd arrived. He looked right and left, but nothing except a spotless white landscape stretched in every direction.

'*She lives all the way up here? All alone? ...For how long?*' He wondered, gazing out at the frozen land.

"Are you surprised?" Laurel asked as she came around the back of the house to stand in the snow in front of him. "A frail young girl like me living all alone high on a mountain with no other houses in sight...crazy, right?"

"I thought it was unusually quiet, but...I never expected this." Alrik replied.

Laurel turned and clasped her hands behind her back as she took a couple of steps toward the edge of the peak to look out at the familiar bird's eye view. "There's actually a village about two miles off the south side of the mountain, but with all this snow, it's almost impossible to see."

"Why don't you live in the village? And where is your family?"

"Well, I used to live in the village, but not long after I was born, my mother and father came down with an unknown illness and died. It spread to several people in the village, and the rumor was that I had caused it somehow, so my grandma took me into the mountains to this cottage. I've lived here ever since."

"You've mentioned your grandmother before. Where is she?"

"She died seven years ago, not long after I turned sixteen...It's just me now."

'She's smiling, but...there's so much sadness behind those eyes. How has she kept going for so long?' Alrik marveled. "Surely, you visit the village."

"I do...about once a month to sell medicine and give treatment to those who need it, but it's not like I have friends or family there." Laurel turned back toward Alrik and twirled around a couple of times, her hair and face sprinkled with snowflakes. "The villagers have many names for me: Laurel the Witch, Mountain Witch, and Witch of the North Wind, just to name a few. Though they're not titles I despise...I'm not very fond of them either. They call me a witch because they don't understand my faith in God. I never understood why, but once the rumors started, there was no stopping them. If I went to the village more often than I do now, it might cause a panic. They might all just pack up and leave...I wouldn't want that. I've caused them enough trouble already."

"I fail to see how you could cause them trouble. From what you told me, it wasn't your fault a sickness spread around. It just happened to be right after you were born. You even treat the sick in the village despite knowing how they feel about you. You have given them the opposite of trouble. If they can't appreciate you, then...then they're blind, ignorant fools!"

"Thank you, Alrik..." Laurel murmured, her eyes softening as her smile widened. "It's been a long time since I've been talked to so kindly."

Something stirred inside Alrik, a feeling he thought he'd never feel for another person ever again. His chest ached, and his heart was pounding against his ribcage, something he never experienced so acutely, even for Marie. He threw the walking stick into the snow and walked--well, more like hobbled-- toward Laurel. He took hold of her shoulders, to steady himself and to make sure he had her full attention, and looked deep into her sapphire blue eyes.

"Laurel, when spring comes and I'm able to walk on my own again, come with me." Alrik suggested. "Little backwoods villages will never appreciate your talent, but in the capital, talents like yours are always needed, and you wouldn't be alone in your faith. There are hundreds who share your beliefs."

"Alrik, that's...that's crazy. I-I can't just leave...My animals, they-" Laurel tried to protest.

"Take them with you. Just please, come with me. I can't leave you here all alone out here." Alrik interrupted.

Laurel's heart fluttered. Her whole body felt light as a feather. She was afraid the slightest gust of wind would lift her off the mountaintop and carry her away.

"I'll...sleep on it." Laurel answered, helping Alrik back to the porch.

"That's all I ask." Alrik replied.

Chapter 6: Breaking Down the Walls

One morning, Alrik awoke extra early. What had awakened him, he had no idea. All he knew was his heart was pounding in his chest, and a few of the things Laurel had told him earlier kept repeating in his ears.

"The parable of the good Samaritan..." Alrik muttered. "I get that she's trying to help me, but why? I'm gruff and stubborn and am not good at being still. How can she put up with me?"

"You know, talking to yourself only makes me think you hit your head way too hard on that step." Laurel's voice commented.

Alrik jumped and sat up. Laurel was standing in the doorway, leaning against the doorframe with her arms crossed and a playful smile on her face.

"How long have you been there?" Alrik

questioned.

"Since about when you started labeling yourself as gruff and rude." Laurel answered. "But to answer your question, I'm not getting by on *my* strength alone. If I did that, I probably would have become the angry herbalist I threatened to become. God gives me the patience and strength to endure hardships. I'm not alone, even all the way up here on this mountain, and I have never been."

"After Marie betrayed me...I walked away from God, and everyone else for that matter. I couldn't trust anyone, and it's been that way for ten years. I'm...not sure I know how to anymore."

Laurel smiled sympathetically and walked over to the bedside table. She pulled open the top drawer and pulled out a Bible. It was covered in dust from lack of use, but it was still in great condition.

"This belonged to my grandmother." Laurel explained, handing the Bible to Alrik. "She lost everything when my parents died, but her faith kept her going and inspired me too. Take some time, read her notes, and pray. God never walks away from us. If you draw near to Him, He will draw near to you."

Alrik hesitantly accepted the brown leather Bible and looked up at Laurel.

"I knew there was something different about you, but at the same time, it was kind of familiar. A man I know, a man I consider my second father, has faith like yours. There's just something about him that makes me want what he has." Alrik murmured.

"He sounds wonderful. I'd love to meet him someday." Laurel replied, turning to leave the room. "Breakfast will be ready soon. Just relax and read until then.

"Thank you..."

"If you need someone to talk to, I'm always here."

Before Alrik could reply, Laurel left the room to prepare breakfast. That left Alrik to his own thoughts, which frightened him more than any battle. Thoughts he thought he buried long ago threatened to resurface.

'Lord, I know it's been a long time, but please...hear my prayer. I need You. I really need You. Help me find wisdom in Your Word again.' Alrik prayed, his eyes squeezed shut. *'I'm*

finally ready to surrender.'

Alrik opened his eyes and turned to his favorite book in the Bible: Psalms. There were Psalms for almost every emotion David had felt: happiness, sadness, shame, doubt, and so many more. Something new always popped out at him.

"For I am poor and needy, and my heart is stricken within me. I am gone like a shadow at evening. I am shaken off like a locust." Alrik read aloud. "Psalm 109: 22-23".

Alrik flipped the worn pages until he came the beginning of Psalm 119.

"How can a young man keep his way pure? By guarding it according to Your word. With my whole heart I seek You; let me not wander from your commandments." Psalm 119:9-10." Alrik continued. "But I have wandered, for ten long years. Yet all this time, the Lord has been with me, protecting me, guiding me. If I were Him, I would have given up on me long ago."

Alrik sat there in silence for a time then flipped back to a passage he used to know by heart many years prior.

"As far as the east is from the west, so far does He remove our transgressions from us. As a father shows compassion on his children, so the Lord shows compassion on those who fear Him. For He knows our frame; He remembers that we are dust." Psalm 103: 12-14" Alrik half-read, half recited from memory.

Alrik paused and let the words sink in for a moment then lifted his thoughts in prayer.

'Lord, I've been so blind. All these years I've been trying to get away from You, but You've been right here with me this whole time.' He paused and took a deep, shaking breath. *'I'm tired of running, of holding onto the hurts of the past, and holding grudges. I'm Yours. Do with me as You will. I'll joyfully do as You command now.'*

Laurel gently knocked on the doorframe, making Alrik open his eyes to look at her. She was holding a tray laden with food. Her smile was warm and understanding, like she was sympathizing with what he was going through.

"I hope I didn't interrupt." She murmured, walking in and setting the tray on the bedside table.

"No, I said what I needed to." Alrik replied, letting out a sigh of relieve as he felt a huge burden he never knew he'd been carrying being lifted off his shoulders. "What happens next is up to God."

"I'm so happy for you!" Laurel exclaimed, placing her small, warm hands on one of his large callused ones. "I was praying for you the entire time I was making breakfast."

"Thank you. I really needed it, and if you don't mind..."

"What is it?"

"Would you keep praying for me?...It's been ten years since the last time I prayed or read the Bible. I'm going to need help."

"I'll do more than that. I'll help you get back into the Word again. We can walk through it together."

"I'd...I'd like that."

A few days passed after Laurel and Alrik began studying the Bible together. Both were benefiting greatly from it, but one day, Alrik felt a tug at his heart. Thoughts of Marie kept popping up in his mind.

"Is something bothering you, Alrik?" Laurel asked from where she sat across the kitchen table from Alrik.

"I...can't seem to get Marie off my mind. It's frustrating. I wish I could just forget her." Arik replied, sighing as he rested his forehead on his hands.

"Marie...That's the girl you mistook me for after your fever caused a nightmare, right?"

"Yes. It's strange. You two are complete opposites, in both looks and personality. I'm not sure how I confused you for her."

"You said she was no one special, but judging by the fact you can't stop thinking about her, makes me thing otherwise."

"She...was my fiancé for a time, many years ago."

"I see...so, I take it she hurt you in some way?"

Alrik released a deep sigh. It wasn't something he wanted to do, but telling Laurel about his past might ease the pain it had left behind.

"Yes. I said I would tell you eventually, but I don't think I should wait any longer. I can't keep dwelling on it."

"That's good that you realize there's a problem. That's the first step to fixing it. I'll help in any way I can."

"Thank you..."

Alrik took a deep breath and related the whole story to Laurel, how he had courted Marie for two years before asking her to marry him. After she became his fiancé, he saw her being kissed by another man two days after telling him she didn't want to marry him.

"Since that day, I never trusted another living soul. I've kept everyone at a distance, even my own family. I played the perfect Christian, but I blamed God for what happened, even though deep down I knew it wasn't true. It was my own fault for being blind to Marie's true nature." Alrik explained.

"I don't think that's the case. You wanted to see the best in Marie. There's no fault in that. We should always try to see the best in people because we're all made in God's image, and if you've accepted Christ into your heart, you're a child of God. We should always try to see others as Christ sees us." Laurel said. "I'm not justifying what Marie did, but it's good that you wanted so badly to see the good in her."

"You may be right, but I made one big

mistake."

"What's that?"

"I never asked her if she was a believer. I was young and foolish. I was only attracted to her beauty. I ignored everything else."

Laurel thought carefully about her response for a moment before replying.

"Maybe it for the best then. I don't like saying that because I know it must have hurt immensely, but I believe God had a better plan for you." Laurel said.

"Looking back on it now, I think you're right. No, I know you're right. It's for the best Marie hurt me the way she did." Alrik agreed.

"It's like the story of Joseph. His brothers sold him into slavery, which was awful, but God turned his terrible situation into a positive one, one that save thousands and thousands of lives, and because Joseph worshiped God no matter what situation he was in, everything he did prospered."

"You know, looking at it from that point of view makes a lot of sense. Sometimes it's necessary to go through bad times."

"Yep. The story of Joseph is one of my

favorites. It hits really close to home."

"What do you mean?"

"Well...the villagers don't exactly make life easy for me. Sometimes I questioned why I stayed here, but then...God brought you to me, someone in dire need. If I had moved away, you probably wouldn't have survived. I'm so glad I stayed here despite all the hardships."

"I guess we can both relate to Joseph. We have very different stories, but at the same time they're very similar."

"That's one of the many amazing things about the Bible. It brings people who may not have anything in common together. That just proves it really is the Word of God."

"I couldn't have said it better myself."

Chapter 7: Setbacks and Tea

A couple of weeks passed. The large piles of snow left by the previous snowstorm had subsided, which allowed Alrik more opportunities to venture outdoors. He felt ridiculous having to use a walking stick just to keep himself upright, but there was no helping it. He had to use it if he didn't want to laze around all day.

"Alrik, don't put so much pressure on your left leg. You have to let it heal a little more first, or you risk it healing the wrong way." Laurel cautioned for what seemed like the tenth time in the last hour as she made her way toward the cottage from the stable with an armload of firewood.

"It's fine. I'm barely using it." Alrik argued, moving toward the porch steps to assist Laurel.

Little did he know, some ice from the previous storm hadn't melted completely on the last step. Before either could react, Alrik's right foot slid out from under him when he placed it on the small patch of ice. With his good leg in the air, the rest of him came crashing backward onto the front steps. His shoulder blades hit first. Then his head hit the top step. He clenched his teeth and hissed in pain.

"Alrik!" Laurel exclaimed, immediately dropping the firewood and running to his side. "Are you all right? What did you hit? Not your shoulder or arm, I hope?"

"No...shoulder blades." Alrik wheezed, as Laurel helped him sit up. "Then my head..."

"Yeah, I think you broke the skin. There's a little blood on the back of your head." Laurel announced after parting his hair to examine the small wound. "I told you to be careful."

"I know."

"You're still not going to listen to me, are you?"

"Probably not."

"Well, the good news is, it didn't scramble your brain. You're still stubborn as a mule."

After getting Alrik back indoors and making sure he hadn't damaged his healing injuries further, Laurel brought the firewood in and threw a few logs into the fireplace, over which an old tea kettle hung whistling quietly.

Laurel removed the kettle from the hook and poured the boiling tea into two cups. Into one she put a few additional herbs to help Alrik heal as quickly as possible and handed it to him. She took the other and sat down to drink it.

Her living area was far from spacious, but it was cozy enough for Laurel. Alrik enjoyed it as well. It was very different from his large manor house, but he felt more at home in the small cottage than he ever did at his own home.

While Alrik and Laurel sat in the living room drinking tea, Snowball sauntered into the room. He walked right up to Alrik and placed his large head on the edge of the chair he was sitting in. Alrik chuckled and patted Snowball's head.

"Where in the world did you find this dog?" Alrik inquired.

"Well, a few years ago, I found him abandoned in a crate in an alley when I went down to the village. He was just a tiny puppy back then." Laurel answered. "He looked like he hadn't eaten in a while. I couldn't just leave him there, so I took him home with me."

"How could those villagers leave a puppy to die? You're very fortunate, Snowball."

"If anyone is fortunate, it's me. I could never have guessed how wonderful he would turn out to be."

Snowball's ears perked up and he ambled over to Laurel. He plopped down in front of her and rested his head in her lap, tail wagging lazily.

"Snowball even saved me from a wolf once." Laurel added, stroking Snowball's soft fur.

"Really? That oversized stuffed animal?" Alrik asked incredulously, raising an eyebrow in disbelief.

"He really did." Laurel assured him. "One night, I stayed out a little later than I should have gathering herbs. On my way back home, I heard movement behind me. By the time I looked around it was too late. A huge silver wolf was only a few feet from me. I panicked and backed up against a tree. Before the wolf could get too close, a deep bark echoed around the snowy forest, sounding more like a crash of thunder than a dog's bark. Then out of nowhere, Snowball burst through the bushes to my left and wedged himself between me and the wolf."

"They didn't fight, did they?"

"No, but they came close. At the last minute, the wolf decided he didn't want to take on Snowball and backed away with his tail between his legs. Since then, even if I stay out a little later than I should, the wolves haven't come near me."

"You really do have yourself an incredible dog."

"I sure do. I thank God for him every day."

Snowball picked his head up from Laurel's lap and rolled over, exposing his fluffy underbelly. He looked at Laurel and then to Alrik with a look that could only mean: "Well, humans? What are you waiting for? Pet me."

"He's just a little bit spoiled though." Laurel giggled.

"There's nothing wrong with that." Alrik replied.

Chapter 8: An Unwelcomed Guest

One morning, after a particularly long snowstorm, Laurel was getting ready to go out to the stable to check on her animals. The harsh winds and heavy snowfall had kept her from tending to them for the last two days. Although she had anticipated this and left extra food, bedding, and blankets for them, she was still anxious to see them.

Alrik had been especially restless the last two days. He paced around the cottage using his walking stick for hours. Laurel was worried he was going to strain his injuries. She constantly had to tell him to sit down and relax or he was going to hurt himself further.

"Alrik, the storm has cleared up. I'm going out to check on the animals." Laurel announced as she slipped on her boots and buttoned up her coat.

"The snow is still deep. Watch your step." Alrik cautioned. "A small girl like you could easily disappear in one of those snow drifts."

"I'll interpret that to mean that you're worried and want me to be careful." Laurel giggled as she opened the door.

Once outside, a sudden gust of icy wind made Laurel bring her scarf up to shield her nose from the cold. As she trudged through the deep snow, there were a few times she thought for sure the wind would pick her up and blow her right off the mountaintop. It was slow going, but she finally reached the stable.

Laurel slid open the door and slipped inside, closing the door behind her to let in as little cold as possible. When they noticed her arrival, the animals looked excited, but something else was making them nervous.

Upon closer inspection of the stable, Laurel noticed what looked like a large ball of fur pressed against the back wall. She cautiously inched closer to get a better look. As she neared, she noticed it wasn't an animal but a man wearing fur garments curled into a ball.

"Oh my! You startled me! What in the world are you doing in here?" Laurel exclaimed.

"S-So...c-cold." The man wheezed, curling tighter into a ball against the wall.

"Wait here for just a minute. I'll go get something to warm you up."

Laurel hurried back to the cottage, running along the flattened areas she had made on her way there. She rushed inside and into the kitchen where there was some leftover oatmeal from breakfast. She poured some into a bowl and dashed out the door once more, barely acknowledging Alrik, who was trying to ask her why she had returned in such a hurry.

When she reentered the stable, the man in the fur was trying to saddle Raj. Not wanting anyone but Laurel to ride him, Raj wasn't making it easy for him.

"Come on now, stupid horse. Hold still!" The man growled, trying to get the bit into Raj's mouth.

Laurel set the bowl on the ground and strode up to the man with her hands on her hips.

"Just what do you think you're doing to my horse?" She demanded.

The burly man turned and looked down at her with beady dark brown eyes. His thick black hair and beard was matted, and his teeth were yellow and cracked. As he looked down at Laurel, his scowl twisted upward into a sinister smirk, and his beady eyes narrowed.

"What does it look like, *woman*? I'm taking your horse, and I have half a mind to take you as well." The man answered, his voice cold and threatening.

The man reached for Laurel's arm, but she avoided his grasp and backed up quickly. When she could back up no further, she felt around for anything she could use as a weapon until her fingers closed around the handle of the pitchfork she used to clear out the hay from the stalls. She pointed it threateningly at the approaching stranger, but her whole body was trembling in fear.

"You're a feisty one, just like the women in my country." Laughed the man, seeming not a bit threatened by the pitchfork. "You'll make great company."

"St-Stay back!" Laurel warned. "I-I'm not afraid to use this!"

"Sure you're not. That's why your hands are shaking." The man chuckled, yanking the pitchfork from Laurel's hands and tossing it aside.

He leaned forward, his face inches from her. His hot, rancid breath making her stomach churn. Laurel's heart pounded in her chest. She had never been that afraid in her entire life. Her mind was racing, trying to figure out a way to escape, but the burly man was blocking all possible escape routes.

'What am I going to do?' Laurel thought desperately, closing her eyes to await the inevitable. *'Father God, please...help me!'*

Chapter 9: Rescue

"I wonder what Laurel was in such a hurry for." Alrik questioned as she followed the path she'd made to the stable.

He was about to open the door when he heard an unfamiliar voice on the other side.

"What's a pretty little thing like you doing alone up here in the mountains?" A male's deep voice asked. "Were you waiting for a man like me to come along and sweep you off your feet?"

Alrik, who had begun toting around his sheathed sword on his back once more, reached for the hilt as he threw open the door. He saw Laurel, her face pale and her blue eyes wide with fear, pinned to the wall by a scraggly-haired burly man wearing fur garments. He gritted his teeth in anger.

'*Barbarian!*' He thought. "Get your filthy

hands off that innocent woman!"

The barbarian, recognizing Alrik's signature red and black longsword, quickly wrapped an arm tightly around Laurel's shoulders and held a dagger to her throat, the cold steel resting against her small neck.

"Draw your sword or take one step closer, and the woman dies!" The barbarian threatened, pressing the dagger so that it broke the skin and a drop of blood trickled down Laurel's neck.

"As expected of a barbarian, always using innocent people to your advantage. No wonder King William wanted you out of Rileni so badly." Alrik spat, his left hand clenched tightly around his walking stick.

"All is fair in love and war." The barbarian replied with a smirk. "And we'll trample over anyone who gets in our way, innocent or not!"

"So tell me, what's a barbarian like you doing in our kingdom? I thought my squadron wiped your lot out."

"I wasn't with my kinsmen when they were annihilated by you Rileni scum. When I came back from scouting, everyone was dead and Rileni soldiers were celebrating. I vowed revenge on Rileni then and there. So, here I am. I'm going to terrorize any village I find until I get to the capital. Then I'll take the head of that arrogant king and parade it back across the river to my kinsmen, and this woman will be my mistress."

"How dare you sully that woman's honor with your foul mouth!"

Without warning, Snowball burst through the doorway, his barking as deep as rolling thunder, and sank his teeth into the barbarian's leg. Using that distraction to his advantage, Alrik threw his walking stick at the Barbarian's head. The barbarian ducked just in time, but by then Alrik had drawn his sword and was approaching fast. Before the barbarian could shake Snowball from his leg, Alrik was on top of him.

He thrust his sword toward the neck of Laurel's captor but stopped just as the point grazed the skin of his neck.

"Let. Laurel. Go." Alrik commanded through gritted teeth. "Or I won't hesitate any longer. Your head will roll before you have time to bat an eye."

The arm that held Laurel fell limp to its owner's side as the barbarian backed up and fled out the back door in fear. Laurel sank to her knees with one hand over the small cut on her neck and eyes wide with fear.

"A-Alrik..." Laurel breathed, her voice barely above a whisper.

Snowball trotted up to her and laid his head and front paws in her lap. He looked up at her with big brown eyes and whined. After watching the barbarian flee into the forest back toward his own land, Alrik knelt next to Laurel.

"Are you all right? He didn't harm you anywhere else, did he?" Alrik asked frantically.

Laurel shook her head, afraid that if she spoke she might burst into tears.

"Let me take a look." Alrik instructed, gently removing Laurel's hand from her neck.

When she pulled her hand back, it was covered in dried blood, but the wound on her throat had stopped bleeding already, due to the pressure she had been applying to it.

"I'm glad it's not any deeper. I thought I might have made it go deeper when I attacked him." Alrik sighed in relief. Laurel remained silent.

Alrik was worried. He had never seen Laurel

look so small and fragile. Her usually bright blue eyes were misty, like she was trying not to cry. Alrik scooted closer and wrapped an arm around Laurel, bringing her closer to him.

"It's all right. He can't hurt you anymore. I promise I won't let anyone else lay a hand on you." Alrik murmured, patting her head comfortingly.

"I...I was so scared." Laurel whispered, still trembling slightly.

"You were braver than anyone else would have been if they were in your place. You didn't even scream when he drew his dagger on you."

"I wanted to, but I was so scared, nothing would come out of my mouth."

"Well, you're safe now, and that's all that matters. Snowball agrees, don't you, boy?"

Snowball wedged himself between Alrik and Laurel and licked both of their noses. Laurel giggled and hugged the giant ball of fluff.

"Thank you, both of you, for saving me." She said. "I-I knew I would be okay. The moment I saw you, I knew God had heard my cry for help."

"All in a day's work for a General Alrik Northstride, servant of the Living God." Alrik replied.

"You didn't strain your injuries trying to save me, did you?"

"No, I'm fine."

Alrik stood up and helped Laurel to her feet, but the second he tried to put pressure on his left leg, it gave out under his weight. He staggered backward and steadied himself against the door of Raj's stall.

"Okay, maybe I overdid it a little bit." Alrik admitted.

Laurel sighed and shook her head as she retrieved Alrik's walking stick.

"What am I going to do with you?" She sighed, not bothering to hide the smile on her face.

Chapter 10: The Village

In the last month of winter before the spring weather set in, Alrik's injuries had healed considerably, so much so that Laurel constantly had to keep at least one eye on the restless general to make sure he didn't do anything to injure himself further. It was, for this reason, she thought taking him to the village with her would be the best way of keeping him out of trouble.

"Alrik, would you like to come to the village with me? It's about the time of the month when I usually pay them a visit." Laurel questioned. "And a think a change of scenery will do you some good."

"That's fine with me. I'll accompany you, if you wish." Alrik replied, twirling his walking stick like a baton with one hand.

"Great, then I'll start getting ready."

Laurel went into the house and packed a bag of medicine and some snacks then went out to the stables. When she entered, both Raj and Stormy whinnied a greeting.

"Sorry, Raj-y boy, but it's Stormy's turn to go to the village this time. I'll take you out when we get back." Laurel chuckled, patting both horses on their soft noses.

Laurel went inside Stormy's stall and grabbed the saddle that was resting on the short wall separating Raj and Stormy's stalls. Since Stormy was already wearing a blanket due to the cool weather, Laurel just plopped the saddle on and tightened the straps. Next, she slipped the bridle on Stormy's head and put the bit in her mouth.

"Alright, ready to go, Stormy-girl?" Laurel asked, patting the mare's shoulder. "This time Alrik will be riding you while I hold the reins."

Stormy bobbed her head as if she understood. Laurel then led Stormy out of the stable and around the front of the house where Alrik was sitting on the front porch. Since Stormy had been the one to carry Alrik when he was injured, she seemed happy that he was doing better. She shoved her large nose in his face and sniffed him.

"Well, hello to you too." Alrik chuckled, stroking her.

"She's happy that you've recovered. You rode on her back to my cottage after I found you that day." Laurel explained.

"Ah, I see. Well, thank you, Stormy."

Again, Stormy bobbed her head as if she understood.

"Well, we better get going. Hop on up." Laurel advised.

Alrik raised an eyebrow at her as if appalled by her statement.

"What? Does your leg still hurt too much?" Laurel questioned.

"No, it's not that. I just refuse to ride if you intend to walk. That would be dishonorable as a general of the Rileni Royal Army." Alrik protested.

"That's sweet, but you're still recovering. Chivalry can wait until you're at your full strength. Besides, the trip will take an hour at most. Do you really think I'm so frail that I can't walk for an hour?" Alrik opened his mouth to reply, but Laurel cut him off. "That was a rhetorical question, but if you're so adamant about it, I'll ride with you on the way back. How does that sound?"

Alrik sighed in defeat. He knew better than to argue with Laurel once her mind was made up. There was no way for him to win against the stubborn herbalist.

"All right, I suppose I can handle that." Alrik relented.

"Good, now let's get going." Laurel replied, smiling triumphantly.

Alrik nodded and placed his right foot in the stirrup. The trouble was going to be getting his left leg over without bumping it. If he put his left foot in the stirrup and swung his right leg over, that would require putting too much pressure on his injured leg. Either way had an undesirable outcome.

"It's might be easier if you ride side-saddle." Laurel suggested.

"You're probably right." Alrik agreed, shifting his position so he could pull himself up easier.

Once he was sitting comfortably in the

saddle, Laurel clipped a saddlebag full of medicine and snacks for the trip onto Stormy's saddle and took the reins.

"Ready?" Laurel asked, looking up at Alrik sitting tall and proud in the saddle.

"Whenever you are." He answered.

"Great, then let's go!"

Laurel led Stormy down the winding mountain. Along the way, Laurel occasionally pointed out her favorite places to gather herbs and other medicinal plants. Alrik didn't speak much. It was not that he disliked the topic of conversation; he just liked listening to the sound of Laurel's voice. When she talked about things she loved, her voice was gentle and sweet. It was like music to his ears.

"There's the village, right up ahead." Laurel announced, snapping Alrik out of his thoughts.

Alrik looked up. He followed Laurel's extended arm toward the horizon and spotted the rooftops of a small village. It was more than a little old fashioned. There were no drainage systems, oil-lit street lamps, or inns like in the larger cities, just houses, a general store, and a blacksmith.

'It's like going back in time one hundred years.' Alrik thought as they approached the outskirts.

As they passed, several villagers eyed them warily and whispered amongst themselves. Alrik strained to hear what they were saying. He caught bits and pieces here and there, but none of it was positive. "Look, Laurel the Witch is back again", "Who's that man with her? I bet she has him under her spell", and "Why won't she just leave us be?" they whispered.

'What nerve!' Alrik scoffed inwardly, then glanced down at Laurel.

Laurel could no doubt hear all of it, but the smile on her face never faltered for an instant. She walked with her head held high down the main road and stopped in front of the general store where she tied Stormy's reins to a hitching post.

Several came forward and inquired about medicine, but they all seemed on edge when speaking to Laurel. Alrik found the whole scene very strange, but Laurel was used to it. It was how they usually treated her. They didn't tell her everything, and they always paid her too much out of fright or just to make her leave sooner.

Some of the younger villagers were more vocal about their dislike of her. They talked in groups and were intentional about their volume when talking about her. Laurel ignored them. A few of their parents had been among the ones taken by the illness when she was born. It was only natural for them to hate her, she always told herself.

"I know she's attractive, but how did she put a man like that under her spell? He looks like a soldier. How could he fall for an evil witch like her?" A particularly loud young man sneered as he passed Laurel as she prepared to leave, making sure he made eye contact with Laurel as he talked.

No matter how often she heard things like that, it was always painful. For a split-second, Laurel's smile faltered. Alrik's battle-train eyes didn't miss it. Without a second thought, he slid from the saddle, and before Laurel could blink, he held the young male off the ground by the collar of his shirt.

"I've had about all I can take of this village's attitude. All of you are petty, spiteful people.

You're ostracizing this innocent girl for something she had nothing to do with because your vision is so clouded by superstition you can't see the truth that's been staring you in the face all this time." Alrik growled.

"So, you trained him to be your attack dog huh, Witch of the North Wind?" The youth spat.

"Silence, whelp! I'm no one's attack dog. I'm General Alrik Northstride of the Rileni Royal Army."

"Tch, yeah right. Even in this backwater village, news still spreads. Alrik Northstride died months ago battling barbarians across the border. You're nothing but an imposter hypnotized by that witch behind you."

"You know nothing about this woman! She is no witch. She used her knowledge of herbs to bring me back from the brink of death because she loves the Lord with all her heart. You will not speak ill of her in my presence."

"Oh, I think I understand now. She's not just a witch, she's an enchantress. She's ensnared you with her charm and feminine wiles."

Alrik's anger was at its limit. He threw down his walking stick and balled his hand into a fist and drew it back, but before he could give the youth a black eye, Laurel placed her small, dainty hand on Alrik's forearm to stop him. Alrik turned his head toward her. She smiled sadly and shook her head, as if saying it wasn't worth it.

"Let's go, Alrik." Laurel murmured.

Alrik sighed and released his grip on the youth's shirt, dropping him on the dusty ground. He picked up his walking stick and climbed back on Stormy without another word.

Laurel packed up the rest of her supplies, untied Stormy, and began heading out of town the way they had come. Once they were a good distance from the village, Laurel climbed into the saddle in front of Alrik and quickened their pace.

"Why..." Alrik whispered. "Why did you stop me? He deserved it for what he said about you!"

"If you had injured him, I'd have to give him medicine for something I could have prevented. Part of my job is to prevent illness and injury beforehand. I couldn't just turn a blind eye because he insulted me. That's unprofessional." Laurel explained, her voice low.

"I wouldn't have injured him too badly..."

"I know, but no matter how small the injury, if I can prevent it, I'm going to. That's what my grandmother would have wanted. She always told me to be like Jesus and turn the other cheek, no matter what the villagers said or did."

Alrik sighed, letting his anger slip away. "You're so calm. Don't their words upset you even a little?"

"Of course, but if I let them get to me, I can't do my job."

"I understand that, but you're a human being just like any of them. Defend yourself! Don't be a doormat for them!"

Laurel was taken aback. No one had ever gotten so angry on her behalf before. She slowed Stormy to a halt before their ascent up the mountain and turned her head to face Alrik who had been glaring at the back of her head since they'd left the village. She smiled brightly up at him.

"Thank you, Alrik." Laurel started. "I'm happy you defended me. I really am. You're the first one since my grandmother to do so."

"I-It was nothing. What kind of general would I be if I didn't defend those who needed it?" Alrik replied, avoiding Laurel's gaze as his cheeks turned pink.

"Not a general of the Rileni Royal Army, that's for sure." Laurel giggled.

Chapter 11: Beneath the Cherry Blossoms

Spring had finally sprung in the mountains of Rileni. The snow from the several snowstorms finally melted, and flowers sprang up from the fresh earth. After more than three long months of winter, it was a welcomed sight, especially for Laurel.

Spring brought back many wonderful memories. It meant that her favorite tree was in full bloom once more. The thought of her cherry tree brought back one memory in particular.

'Granny, how old is this cherry tree? Do you know?' A small seven-year-old Laurel asked as she and her grandmother sat beneath the sea of pink petals.

'It's been here as long as we've lived on this mountain, Laurel honey, and I'm sure many

years before that.' Her grandmother, Rosemary Meyers, replied as she opened up her brown leather Bible.

While Rosemary had been talking, little Laurel had climbed up to the lowest branch of the Cherry tree. She sat on the branch and looked out at the land before her then down at her grandmother.

'Look, Granny! I'm Zacchaeus!" Laurel called, swishing her dangling legs back and forth from her perch.

'Well, Zacchaeus, you come down.' Her grandmother chuckled. 'I've got a Bible story for you.'

Laurel's big blue eyes lit up, and her smile widened. She nimbly scrambled down the trunk of the tree and returned to her grandmother's side.

'Is it Noah's ark? Or Jonah and the whale? Or Jesus walking on water?" Laurel aske eagerly, eyes wide with wonder.

'No, today I'm going to read a story you've probably never heard of. It's about a man from the Old Testament named Balaam and his talking donkey.' Rosemary answered.

'Really?! A talking donkey?! Did that really happen?'

'It really did. Everything in the Bible is true and really happened, even the talking donkey.'

'That's so amazing! God can do anything, can't he, Granny?'

'He most certainly can, my sweet little Laurel. He most certainly can.'

That was one of Laurel's fondest memories. From a very young age, Laurel's grandmother had read the Bible to her and helped foster a faith in her that continued to grow, even after her death.

"It's that time of year again...Alrik should be fully recovered soon." Laurel murmured to herself as she washed the dishes from that morning's breakfast. "I guess it's about time I gave him my answer."

Laurel finished washing the last dish and walked out to the front porch where Alrik usually spent his time.

"Alrik, I want you to see something. Come with me?" Laurel asked.

Alrik, who had almost completely recovered from his injuries, looked up from where he was sitting playing fetch with Snowball

"Sure. Is it far?" Alrik replied, slowly getting to his feet.

"Nope, not far at all." Laurel answered.

Even though Alrik could walk without the help of the walking stick, it was slow going. His left leg was weak from lack of use, so Laurel had him go walking with her whenever the unpredictable mountain weather would allow, but there was one place she had purposefully avoided taking him until that day: The cherry tree.

Laurel walked closely beside Alrik, always making sure to keep a close eye on him. His injuries had healed remarkably well, but she just wanted to make sure he didn't overdo it. Over the last couple of months, he'd overdone it on many occasions.

Alrik gave her a quizzical look when they didn't take their usual path around the peak of the mountain. Instead, they descended a bit and took a right at a fork in the road. Then before the path ended, Laurel stopped and veered off the dirt path and onto a well-worn trail through the grass and foliage.

Alrik followed, wondering what in the world Laurel had planned. After about five minutes, sunlight was shining through the tree line in front of them. When he stepped past the natural barrier of bushes and thick foliage along the path, his eyes widened in surprise and wonder.

"It's beautiful..." Alrik breathed as he looked at the cherry tree in full bloom. "I've never seen anything like it."

"This cherry tree has been my favorite place ever since I was small. I wanted to bring you to a special place, so I could...give you my answer." Laurel explained, gently placing her hand on the trunk of the tree as she stood on one of its' large exposed roots, looking up into the sea of pink blossoms. "A while back...you asked me to come with you when you recovered. I've kept quiet about it, but I knew the answer the moment you asked. At the same time, I needed time, time to pray and think about your offer. Now I know what God wants for me."

Alrik's heart was pounding in his chest. From the tone of her voice, he thought she was going to decline. The fear of leaving her to fend for herself gnawed at him from the inside.

"Laurel, please, you don't have to stay here alone. Come with me. I'll provide for you. You won't have to worry about anything ever again." Alrik pleaded.

"Alrik, you didn't let me finish." Laurel giggled. "I've decided...I'll come with you. To be honest...after having you to talk to these past three and a half months, I don't think I could go back to living alone. You helped me remember my love of interacting with humans who don't despise me and that my life is valuable because I'm a child of God...Thank you."

"...I should be the one thanking you. You've done nothing but help me these past months, even though at first I fought you tooth and nail. I wouldn't be alive if it weren't for you, and...you helped me rekindle my faith in Christ and trust other people again. After Marie betrayed me and ran into the embrace of another, I closed my heart off from God and the rest of the world, but you...somehow wormed your way into it and broke down the walls I'd build around my heart from the inside out...Thank you, Laurel."

Laurel smiled as a gust of wind stirred the air around them, sending pale pink petals in every direction. Alrik returned the smile and gently lifted her from her perch on the tree's roots and set her on the grass in front of him.

"But there's one other thing I'd like to ask you."

Chapter 12: The General Returns

The capital of Rileni was a bustling city full of lively people. On the north side of the city was the castle, home of Rileni's reigning monarch, King William Armand V. It was toward this castle that Alrik and Laurel were headed.

The busy streets made it a slow journey, especially since they were using a covered wagon to transport all of Laurel's animals and belongings. Even with both Raj and Stormy pulling the wagon, the crowds would barely part to let them pass.

While Alrik drove the wagon, Laurel looked around at the capital city in awe. There were so many new sights, sounds, and smells. Never in her life had she ever been to such a large city or seen so many people. It was all so exciting but terrifying at the same time.

"You look a little overwhelmed." Alrik observed as they sat motionless at an intersection full of people trying to get to their destinations.

"Maybe a little..." Laurel admitted, resting a hand on Snowball's head. "I've never seen so many people in my life."

"Don't worry. Once we get closer to the castle, the crowds will thin out."

"That's good. It's going to take me a little while to get used to such a large city."

Alrik smiled warmly at Laurel "I'm sure it won't take you very long."

Laurel smiled back. "I'm glad you think so."

"Alrik, is that you?" A familiar, sickly-sweet voice asked.

Alrik stiffened. He knew that voice anywhere, and it was one he never thought he would hear again. He turned his head to the right and saw none other than Marie standing there, just feet from him.

"Hello, Marie." Alrik greeted stiffly. "How have you been?"

"Alrik, it is you! I heard you were killed by barbarians trying to protect Rileni." Marie replied. "How in the world did you survive?"

"It's a long story, Marie. I need to get to the castle to report to King William."

"Of course, of course. When you get done though, you should come see me."

"Sorry, Marie. I'm not interested."

Marie blinked in surprise. Then she noticed Laurel sitting in the wagon behind Alrik. "And who is this?"

"This is Laurel Meyers. She found me when I was badly injured and took care of me until I was fully recovered."

"Hello, Laurel! It's *lovely* to meet you!" Marie greeted, over-dramatically.

"Hello. It's lovely to meet you as well." Laurel replied, doing her best to be friendly.

"So, Alrik, I feel simply *awful* about what happened before. Won't you give me another chance?"

"I forgive you, Marie, but I can't marry you." Alrik said.

"Why not?" Marie demanded, anger flashing in her dark eyes.

"Because Laurel is going to be my wife."

Marie's eyes widened in shock, and she

whipped her head back toward Laurel, who was hugging Snowball closer to her out of nervousness.

"You chose this common *girl* over a noblewoman like me? Are you *blind*?" Marie spat.

"You had your chance, Marie." Alrik continued, urging the horses onward since the road had cleared up. "I'm sorry, but I've moved on."

And without another word, Alrik and Laurel rode down the street toward the castle, where King William lived.

After the supposed death of his prized general, Alrik Northstride, the king had fallen into a melancholy state. He'd seen real potential in Alrik and hoped to nurture his talent by mentoring him as a father would his son.

"Your highness! A person claiming to be General Alrik Northstride has asked for an audience with you!" One of the attendants announced upon entering the throne room.

King William immediately jolted from his slouched position.

"Let him in." He commanded. "I will see

him immediately."

"Yes, your highness." The attendant replied with a bow and left the room.

'Could it really be Alrik? He disappeared over three months ago. The only thing his squadron found was his helmet on the riverbank.' the king thought.

His thoughts were soon interrupted by the large, ornate doors of the throne room opening again. Though his vision had begun to fail him in his old age, he could tell by the sound of the footsteps, and the way the man carried himself that it was no imposter.

"Your highness, you have my deepest apologies." Alrik began, getting on one knee and bowing his head. "Though I heard from the people of the capital of my squadron's victory, I cannot take credit. I was caught off guard by a sudden explosion and fell into the river, utterly shameful for a general of Rileni. I beg your forgiveness."

The king rose from his throne and descended the steps to meet Alrik. He placed his hands on Alrik's shoulders and brought him back to a standing position.

"General Alrik Northstride, you need not bow nor should you apologize. You led your squadron to victory over the Barbarians of the North. I read the reports and talked to many eyewitnesses. You were there up until the very end." The king protested. "More importantly, what happened to you, my boy? Where have you been, and who is this young lady with you?"

Laurel, flustered at being put on the spot by such a powerful individual, bowed her head and curtsied with shaking legs.

"I am no one special, your highness." Laurel answered, voice quiet.

"She's being modest, your highness." Alrik corrected. "It's because of this young woman I am standing before you today."

"Oh?" The king questioned. "Please explain. I must know how you survived."

"After the blast from a nearby explosive, I tumbled into the river, not without injury, and lost consciousness for a time. When I awoke, I had washed up on the banks of the river somewhere. I used my sword to drag myself out of the water, but after a few feet, I could go no further. This young woman, who lived in the mountains in the Northeast found and took me back to her home. She is an herbalist and a good one at that. She treated my wounds, gave me new clothes, and prepared hot meals. And above all, it's because God led me to her that my faith in Him has been renewed. He worked through her to find his very stubborn lost sheep. It's because of her kindness, I am fully healed, physically and spiritually."

"That's wonderful, Alrik! And what is your name, young one?" the king asked, looking to Laurel.

"Laurel Meyers, your majesty." Laurel answered, bowing again.

"Laurel...a lovely name. If I may ask, what were the extent of General Northstride's injuries."

"His physical injuries were numerous. He had a broken tibia, a fractured radius, and his left shoulder popped out of the socket. Since he fell into the river during early winter, he suffered from some of the effects of hypothermia as well."

"My...It's a miracle he survived!"

"Yes. I was surprised as well. He has a strong will to live, but I believe that God wasn't through with him and brought him to me. I can't take credit for God's work."

"Strong will is an understatement." The king chuckled. "I'm sure he wasn't a very cooperative patient at first, was he?"

"Cooperative as a mule at first, your majesty." Laurel answered, amusement dancing in her eyes as Alrik looked away in embarrassment when the king laughed heartily. "But I managed, with a little prayer and threatening him with a longer recovery period if he didn't do as he was told, that is."

"Miss Meyers, thank you for helping my most loyal general. I am in your debt."

"O-Oh, no, your majesty. I-I just did what I believed God was telling me to do. I-I don't deserve such praise."

"Come now. Saving a general's life is no small feat. If you should desire anything, if it is within my power to give it to you, I will." The king then turned back to Alrik. "As for you, you will be resuming your duties as one of my generals, won't you?"

"If your highness desires me to do so, then I would be honored." Alrik answered, bowing his head respectfully.

"Very good. I'm overjoyed to have you back!"

"I must ask one thing before that, however."

"And that is...?"

"I know I've been absent for over three months, but I must ask for another small leave of absence."

"May I ask the reason?"

"I'm going to make Laurel Meyers my wife." Alrik put his arm around Laurel's shoulder and drew her closer to his side.

The king was overjoyed. Since Alrik had become a general, the king had gotten to know him on a personal level. He could see the deep hurt in Alrik's eyes, and he could see how he kept everyone at arm's length. He never let anyone get too close.

King William was worried for the young man. He was too young to be so distrusting of others, but he could see the change in Alrik's eyes. The hurt and pain that once filled them was gone, and in their place, was something totally new --kindness and affection.

However, there was still one issue, one that the king must press before making his decision.

Chapter 13: The King's Offer

"Alrik, as you know, I have no children of my own, and my wife died long ago. I have no hope of an heir. That is why, after I am gone, I was considering passing the crown on to you." King William began. "I see real potential in you, and I'd hate for you stay on the front lines your entire life. What do you say, General Northstride? Will you accept the crown when it comes my time to go?"

"Your majesty...I couldn't possibly..." Alrik tried to protest.

"Why? You're more than qualified. You're a superb leader. Everyone in the kingdom respects you as a general and as a person. You would be a king loved by the people." King William reasoned.

"Are you certain? You really want me to be

next in line for the throne?"

"I am."

Laurel could scarcely believe her ears. Before her very eyes, the stubborn General Northstride had been offered the crown. Something was amiss though.

"Laurel, did you hear that? You're going to be the queen of this country one day." Alrik announced, eyes bright with happiness and excitement.

"Just a moment. As the next in line for the throne, you must marry someone of noble blood. I won't allow just anyone to be the next queen." King William protested.

Alrik's eyes widened in shock. In the last five minutes, he'd been offered the crown but denied of marrying the woman he loved.

"If that's the case, your majesty...I must decline." Alrik stated firmly.

"Alrik, what are you doing?" Laurel whispered. "You're turning down this once in a lifetime opportunity!"

"Laurel, I love you. If marrying you means staying a general for the rest of my life, I will gladly do it."

"Now, now, don't be so hasty, Alrik." King William interrupted. "I haven't finished." He turned to Laurel and smiled kindly. "Young lady, do you have any family to speak of?"

"I don't, your majesty. My last remaining family member died seven years ago." Laurel answered.

"Miss Laurel, as I said earlier, I have no children of my own. If you're willing, I'd like to adopt you as my own daughter. You bear a striking resemblance to my late wife."

Again, Laurel couldn't believe her ears. King William Armand V was offering to adopt her as his own daughter, making her the princess of Rileni.

"Your majesty, I'm just a girl from a village in the middle of nowhere, and even there I was an outcast. I'm not worthy of such a title." Laurel protested humbly.

"My dear, you've shown great kindness to one of my most trusted companions. I can't let that go unrewarded. However, even if Alrik had brought you to me, without you having shown him great kindness, I would still have offered. The fact that Alrik was willing to refuse the crown if it meant not marrying you says volumes about you. He doesn't trust others easily, as you probably already know."

"Yes...Your majesty, are you absolutely certain you want me as your daughter?"

"I am. You would make this old king very happy."

"You're too kind, your majesty." Laurel whispered, tears welling in the corners of her eyes.

King William reached out and took both of Laurel's hands in his large wrinkled ones. "Please, call me father."

Laurel nodded, afraid that if she spoke, she would dissolve into tears.

"Alrik, you won't mind postponing the wedding for a bit, would you?" King William asked. "I'd like some time to get know the daughter God has given me in my old age."

"I would wait forever, your majesty." Alrik answered, smiling lovingly at Laurel. "After all, I love her."

"I love you too, Alrik." Laurel murmured. "With all my heart."

Acknowledgements

I want to say a special thank you to my Journalism teacher Dr. Stan Brooke. He took the time to read over my unfinished manuscript and even gave me some very helpful feedback. I couldn't have made the book as long as it is without his help.

I also want to say thank you to all my friends and family who have supported me all along the way, whether it was reading my manuscript and giving feedback or just encouraging me along the way. I wouldn't have had the confidence to publish this book without them.

All the Bible verses I used were from the Crossway English Standard Version.

About the Author

My name is Lexie Hobby. I am currently a senior at a private high school. I've loved reading and writing for a long time now. My favorite book genres are historical fiction and fantasy, so I thought: 'Why not combine them?', and that's when the idea for *Thyme for Change* popped in my head.

I was born with a genetic disorder called Albinism. It effects the pigment producing genes, causing my skin and hair to be much lighter than normal and effects my vision. I am considered legally blind in both eyes, even with my glasses.

For a long time, I struggled with this, even after I accepted Christ as my Savior. I was stubborn and prideful. However, being stubborn isn't always a bad thing. I never let anyone tell me I couldn't do something just because of my vision. I wrote this book for two main reasons.

The first is, I wanted to put my God-given talents to good use, and second, I wanted to prove that just because I have a disability, doesn't mean God can't use me.

Thyme for Change

www.ingramcontent.com/pod-product-compliance
Lightning Source LLC
Chambersburg PA
CBHW021929170626
46807CB00007B/3033